GHOST HUNTERS

Edited By Wendy Laws

First published in Great Britain in 2021 by:

Young Writers
Remus House
Coltsfoot Drive
Peterborough
PE2 9BF
Telephone: 01733 890066
Website: www.youngwriters.co.uk

Printed and bound in the UK by BookPrintingUK
Website: www.bookprintinguk.com
YB0487H

FOREWORD

Enter, Reader, if you dare...

For as long as there have been stories there have been ghost stories. Writers have been trying scare their readers for centuries using just the power of their imagination. For Young Writers' latest competition Spine-Chillers we asked pupils to come up with their own spooky tales, but with the tricky twist of using just 100 words!

They rose to the challenge magnificently and this resulting collection of haunting tales will certainly give you the creeps! From friendly ghosts and Halloween adventures to the gruesome and macabre, the young writers in this anthology showcase their creative writing talents.

Here at Young Writers our aim is to encourage creativity and to inspire a love of the written word, so it's great to get such an amazing response, with some absolutely fantastic stories.

I'd like to congratulate all the young authors in this collection - I hope this inspires them to continue with their creative writing. And who knows, maybe we'll be seeing their names alongside Stephen King on the best seller lists in the future...

CONTENTS

Ashleigh Hudspith (13)	54	Albert Mattingly (13)	83
Hollie Hickman (13)	55	Sasha Turner (13) & Martha	84
Kenan Catchpole-Mateu (12)	56	Millie Bray (13)	85
Ramero Shepherd (13)	57	Evie Basher (12) & Charlotte	86
Kieran Wyatt (13)	58	Laurie Messam (12)	87
Olivia Kirkhoff (11)	59	Molly Howard (13)	88
Max Allen (14)	60	Tyler Davies (12)	89
Freddy Chapman (15)	61	Seren Jones (11)	90
		Etienne Pinto (13)	91

Barnwell School Upper School, Stevenage

Shanira Hardy (13)	62
Hanifa Ashraf (14)	63
Anisa Ashraf (14)	64

Benedict Biscop CE Academy, Moorside

Tiffany Nell (11)	65

Birkenhead School, Oxton

Ellora Chatwin (12)	66

Bishopston Comprehensive School, Bishopston

Samuel Martin (12)	67
Sophie Mather (13)	68
Harriet Fox (12)	69
Anna Martin (12)	70
Manon Lythgoe (11)	71
Emily Taylor (13)	72
Daniel Adams (15)	73
Hollie Davies (12)	74
Liv Thomas (12)	75
Sienna Warren (12)	76
Evie Manning (13) & Poppy Harry-Thomas	77
Tehillah Thomas (12)	78
Phoebe Holt (14)	79
Ioan Marvelley (13)	80
Chloe Marfell (11)	81
Tristan Crocker (14)	82

Toby Hulatt (13)	92
Jack Arnold (12)	93
Sonny Curtis (13)	94
Amelia Griffiths (13) & Eden	95
Anna Williams (13)	96
Emily Brown (13) & Lara Edwards	97
Lucca Benjamin Smith (14)	98
Eres Parry (13)	99
Esther Harman-Cashmore (12)	100
Jake Cowell (13)	101
Phoebe Jago (12)	102
Mali Gregory (12)	103
Leyah Nicholls (12)	104
Megan Richards (11)	105
Libby Hale (12)	106
Molly Jones (12)	107
Luke Norman (13)	108
Samuel Eadon-Crosby (12)	109
Livvy Brereton (12)	110
Reuben Cain (14)	111
James Hornsby-Smith (13)	112
Fern Thompson (12)	113
Harry Lewis (12)	114
Charlotte Brady (13)	115
Aedan Mackenzie (14)	116

Chetwynde School, Barrow-In-Furness

Poppy Tyson (13)	117
Nathan Lee Cheong (13)	118
Liam Crawshaw (13)	119
Hannah Lauderdale (13)	120
Chloe Birt-Reed (12)	121

The Berwickshire High School, Langtongate

THE MINI SAGAS

REBORN ONCE AGAIN

Isabella and I liked going out to the woods. One rainy Sunday, we went for a walk in the woods. Thunder struck! Isabella screamed. "It's just thunder!" I yelled, without turning around. She never replied. I turned around. "Isabella, where are you?" I shrieked!

I flashed home, thumping against the door, illustrating to Isabella's mum what'd happened. She rushed with me and we went to the woods to look for her.

We stood at the exact co-ordinate of where the event occurred. We found nothing but a decrepit doll that seemed an awful lot like Isabella. Lightning struck once more...

Reeha Rifdhy (12)
Al Aqsa Secondary School, Leicester

THE MACABRE WEDDING

A melodic, high-pitched hum became unmistakeably louder; she was approaching nearer and nearer to annihilate the wedding. Why, just why didn't I pay my respects and lay flowers on her grave? Mary Whiddon was clearly visible now, in her pristine white wedding dress, gliding along with an eerie and pearly glow to her. While I breathed my almost certain last breaths, I pondered on how this zealous ghoul would put an end to my life; strangle me? Execute me? How inequitable of this ghost to murder a bride because she was murdered a few minutes after her wedding commenced?

Hafsa Rehman (11)
Al Aqsa Secondary School, Leicester

THE WALKING DEAD

As Isabella marched through the creepy graveyard to visit the grave of her dead grandparents, all her fears shivered down to her spine. Having no idea that a hand was going to grab her feet and take her with it into the barren ground. Little did she know all her fears were going to come to life. As she marched into the darkness of the graveyard the ground was starting to sink, she knew what was going to happen next. She ran but it was too late. All that was heard from her was her screams yelling for help.

Sara Shokry (12)
Al Aqsa Secondary School, Leicester

ONCE A YEAR

One day a year, when the night is the coldest, a man takes off from his workshop as his sleigh creaks. The flakes of white land on his neck as he lands on your roof. He looks down your pitch-black chimney and sees that your fire is dead. He crawls down into your living room as the chilling air fills it. He sees a tree of green with dim lights surrounding it and places boxes of unknown items underneath. He hears a noise and quickly slithers back up the chimney. The man in red and white flees the scene.

James Parker
All Saints Catholic High School, Kirkby

WHY DID IT HAVE TO BE JEREMY?

It was Halloween, I had planned the prank for weeks. The door would close and lock us in, Jeremy and I would jump at the projected shadows dancing up the walls and then he would scream at the tomato ketchup I had used as blood. But when I got home from work the door was already open.

"Jeremy," I called.

No reply.

The door creaked as it shut behind me.

"Jeremy," I called again.

No reply.

I saw a shadow dart across the ceiling.

"Jerem-" I didn't need to finish my sentence, the blood that covered his body said everything.

Beth Nevitt (15)

Alleyne's Academy, Stone

TEARS OF THE NIGHT

I stand there alone in the dead of night. The only noise I can hear is my tears slowly dropping to the floor. Then I see a faint glimmer of a figure standing behind me. Threatening me with a knife, threatening me with my life. My heart bursts. He lifts the knife. I fall. Darkness surrounds me. The tears rise, forming a spiral around me trapping me within its clutches. Lonely. Afraid. Timorous. A slight glimmer of hope transcends me into a dream. A minuscule gap opens getting bigger by the second. It stops. Do I dare look behind...?

Eloïse Rawsthorne-Durand (14)
Alleyne's Academy, Stone

MISSING

"Holly, are you coming out tonight?" Charlie questioned her down the phone.

"I'll be at yours soon," she replied enthusiastically.

Charlie sat waiting at the door, there was a knock. He opened the door. They walked for miles until they finally found an abandoned house. "Let's go in," Holly whispered nervously. They pushed open the door and quietly went inside. It was cold, Holly turned to ask Charlie a question, he wasn't there... Holly turned back, there was a staircase. Something touched her. "Charlie? Is that you?" She didn't hear anything. There was a flash of lightning. Darkness.

Bethany Davison (13)
Aylesford School, Aylesford

DARK FIGURE

Dark moonlight bouncing off puddles on the road, I walk down the street behind my house. *Rustle!* Something in the bushes? I turn around. Someone there? I start to walk faster. Faster and faster. There are footsteps behind me. Closer and closer. Run faster. Run faster. My sight's going, going, going... darkness. Light... I'm waking up. There's no one here. Only a dark figure staring at me. Is it alive? Am I alive? I can't tell. I start to panic. The longer I panic the closer it gets. *Blink.* Closer. *Blink.* Closer. *Blink.* It's right next to me...

Rose Weller (13)
Aylesford School, Aylesford

LATE NIGHT STROLL

"What's over here?" yelled Ava, as she was heading for darkness. Cleo followed behind. They crept forwards into the shadows. The eerie sounds whispered around them. Behind the mist stood an ancient castle.

"Oh my!" exclaimed Cleo. The astonishment struck their faces. They stumbled closer to it reluctantly, both glanced at one another. Out of nowhere, a light shone through one of the dirty windowpanes. The two girls gazed to see a shadow amongst the light. It was swiftly moving across the room. A bolt of lightning hit the forest behind them. Ava turned her head...

Imogen Parry (13)
Aylesford School, Aylesford

THE ABANDONED ASYLUM

"Stop Jamie! You know you're not allowed in there!"
exclaimed Peter.
"I know!" he shouted back.
As soon as Jamie entered he saw different graffiti all over
the walls. Out of nowhere, a sinister spine-chilling scream
echoed through the asylum. In the blink of an eye, a creepy
clown jumped out of a room with a large machete. Jamie
jumped up in the air and started sprinting out of the asylum.
As he ran he heard an ear-piercing laugh that made him run
faster than ever. Jamie bolted past Peter. Peter looked at
the clown and ran.

Martin Nikolov (11)
Aylesford School, Aylesford

RUNNING

I run through the creaky door. The branches hit the window viciously. The howls of the ghosts call loudly. Malevolence and terror, the glare of evil faces. Violently, the wind bangs the door shut. In all different areas to confuse the devilish creatures. In the distance, music starts to play. I feel my eyes circling around the room. Water drips from the tap in the room opposite. *Crunch! Crunch!* My foot stood on leaves that had blown in. My heart's pounding with terror. Sweat drips down my face as I run away. The devil chases me...

Evelyn Open (13)
Aylesford School, Aylesford

BLACK WOLF

All the lights went out, including the flashlights. The air became cold and thin, none of us could move. We were frozen with fear. Then on the other side of the corridor was a thud. Tom yelled, "Hello... is anyone there?" He walked forward. We were all walking towards the noise, calling out to the thud, but when we were at the end of the corridor we received a reply... an unholy snarl coming from the room next to us. Luckily there was a small window on the door, we peeked through and saw the unnatural orange eyes staring back...

Caiden Dilks (13)
Aylesford School, Aylesford

DIRECTIONS

The owls howled as my spine shivered. The cold air hit me like a wave. I waited by a bench to calm my paranoia. An old car stopped at my side. "Do you know directions to the nearby church?" the mysterious man questioned. I stepped over to his car.

"Yeah, keep going and turn left," I replied generously, giving the man a warm smile. His eyes turned a crimson red as I felt the same shivering feeling. "Are you okay?" I asked frightened. The next thing I saw was gleaming lights and my head hit the pavement.

Izzy McNally (13)
Aylesford School, Aylesford

DREAM

As I walked up the stairs to the abandoned house I got more nervous, every second. I carefully opened the door and walked around the first room. I walked into one of the bedrooms and saw a little girl's dusty, broken bed, but something stuck to me... The closet door was open and in the slightest crack, there was something... "Argh!" I screamed as I sat up from the horrible nightmare. I sat for a moment and calmed down. I looked at my closet door. It was slightly open and there was a hand appearing from the crack...

Isabella Pelling (13)
Aylesford School, Aylesford

HOUSE IN THE GRAVEYARD

It was a cold, dark night when we saw an abandoned house in the middle of a graveyard. There were creepy, cold, iron gates at the entrance, we walked into the house. The door was unlocked so Jeff and I walked in. We looked around, then Jeff shouted, "I've found some stairs." I ran to his voice, he was already climbing the stairs. All of a sudden the stairs disappeared beneath him and he fell. They reappeared. I continued up the stairs and saw a door. I opened it and there he stood. I saw it... "Help!"

Jack Hickinson (13)
Aylesford School, Aylesford

FOOTSTEPS AND SOUNDS

As I jogged through the dark silent night the footsteps followed. When I slowed down, they slowed down, I sped up, they sped up. Panic filled me and I started to sprint, though the thousands of massive trees made very difficult obstacles. I managed to block out the footsteps with my heavy breathing. Suddenly, out of the corner of my eye, I saw a black silhouette glaring at me. I used the last of my energy to run, hopefully escaping the forest. It wasn't enough. Next thing I knew I was safe at home, but who took me?

Ella Rollinson Small (13)
Aylesford School, Aylesford

A CHURCH WALK

I was out with my friends and it was gloomy and dark. We decided to explore the church that everyone had said was haunted. The closer and closer we got we could hear screams of help coming from inside. The trees standing at the side looked like bodyguards. Strangely, the door opened, we decided to go in. Cobwebs were hanging everywhere. Walking further in, I felt more anxious. We went upstairs to the bell. Everyone was gathered talking and while standing near the edge of the tower I felt myself being nudged...

Emily Open (13)
Aylesford School, Aylesford

THE HONEYMOON

I could see it, ready to jump. Paralysed, in a state of fear. My wife and I found a low budget cabin for our honeymoon. After a long journey, we had finally arrived. Dropping everything off we headed down to the beach. After hours we headed back hand in hand. To our surprise the door was open. Noises rattled the walls. Heading to our room my legs started shaking. A shadow stood awaiting my approach. I could see it, ready to jump. Paralysed in a state of fear, I stepped into the cabin...

Isabelle Milligan (13)

Aylesford School, Aylesford

THE MAN

I woke up and gave a yawn, I was woken by the wind wildly brushing through my hair. "I thought I closed that window." I moved over and shut the window, there was a man in my room holding a bloody knife. I gave a big gulp, getting ready to scream. He stretched out to me and stopped me before I could move a muscle. I elegantly dashed for the door, stamping on toys. The house was hushed, I went into my parents' room. Not there! Brother not there! Dog not there..!

Nathan Jull (12)
Aylesford School, Aylesford

THE TALL MAN

It was a normal evening, yet the entire day had felt off. I dragged myself through the front door and turned on my lights that flickered as I threw my bag onto my sofa. I sat down and slid my shoes off. I decided to go upstairs, as I did I felt a warm breath on my neck. I turned abruptly, yet saw nothing. I thought nothing of it. I continued to my room yet only had my dim lamp to light it. That's when I saw him towering over me with intimidating, blank eyes...

Ali Knell (13)
Aylesford School, Aylesford

GIBBINORT

"Staraan, describe the planet you're from," the scientist muttered, after finally encasing Staraan into the cold leather bed.

"It's a beautiful planet, mister," Staraan said softly and dreamily, her coiled, turquoise hair flowing and waving to the breeze of the cool air. "It's called... Gibbinort." Staraan's eyes glowed a bloody, eerie red. She suddenly screamed like a tremendous monster, her cry louder than the howls of a million beasts. One second. One second was all it took for the roar of Staraan's voice to blast the terrified scientist to intergalactic space and let her escape back to her home... Gibbinort.

Kamila Soltysik (14)
Barnwell Middle School, Shephall Green

SILENCE IS DEADLY...

The floorboards creaked. He wasn't alone. Someone else was there, looking for him. *Bang! Bang! Bang!* They were pounding on the door two away from him. Any moment now, the person would come barging in and find him. There goes more banging. One door away. Lynx blew his candle out and hid in the corner furthest from the door. Quietly, the handle twisted, revealing a black figure storming in. This unknown figure started destroying everything. They knew Lynx was there. "Come out from the shadows, kid." Lynx closed his eyes, praying he'd leave. Silence fell. Where had the figure gone...?

Sarah Notley (14)
Barnwell Middle School, Shephall Green

LONDON BRIDGE BRUTALITY

Streetlights flickered as I walked past. Puddles dampened my shoes. My torn shirt was asking to be ripped. *Ding-dong!* Big Ben struck midnight. I felt something brush my shoulder. My heart ran out of my traumatised body.

"Hello," something whispered. The mysterious object pushed me towards London Bridge. I felt demons rebelliously fighting to be in command inside my head. Finally, I was possessed by raging demons.

The demons gave in, but I was too busy falling down the bridge like a paraglider. *Splash!* I hit the water. I felt as heavy as a whale. Did I drown?

Joshua Beedell (13)
Barnwell Middle School, Shephall Green

WHAT A HORRIBLE JOKE

I hated this place. The obstreperous planks, the hideous, archaic furniture and the sinister shadows across the room. I despised ghost hunting, but the pay was good. Risking your life to find information about a banshee... What a joke. I clutched my hand down on the lantern handle, walking into the gloomy, abandoned school. Ignoring weak, feeble whispers, I sluggishly stepped into the slovenly cafeteria. Broken lights flickered rapidly as an ear-piercing shriek echoed through the lonely, ruined school. Panic crashed over my body like a tsunami. Rotten, sharp nails dug into my side. I screamed...

Jasmin Carvatchi (14)
Barnwell Middle School, Shephall Green

THE STREETS

The silence fell across the dark street, lamp posts flickering in the night. Everything was dull, but at the same time creepy. The eerie silence, the flickering light amongst the occasional screech of a crow. Nothingness, but everything-ness, emptiness but fullness. And then... a screech of a crow soaring through the cold air, ready to lose its sight of the world, it stopped in mid-air, then it fell. Falling to the ground, the crow screeched again and again. The silence became deadly screeching. No, the night became deadly screeching. And that's what the wretched night is about.

Harry Galer (13)
Barnwell Middle School, Shephall Green

COLD WINTER'S NIGHT

There once was a legend about a girl who wanted everything. The house she lived in was pristine with a dark enigma of unexplainable deaths hidden inside its walls. This woman's name was Evelyn.

One night when the thunder was crashing outside Evelyn was eating. The lights went out. This phenomenon was known to happen quite rarely around here but then Evelyn still sat at the table in shock, felt something or someone brush her shoulder. It felt like death brushing her shoulder. Thunder struck again. Evelyn turned in horror when she saw it. Pure fear ran through her...

Archie Parry (13)
Barnwell Middle School, Shephall Green

SACRIFICED

Death. Life. The voices in her head replaying like 'trick or treat' on Halloween. Her pupils, blood-red and dilated as if hell was coming to grab her. Her sallow yellow skin screaming for mercy as torture ripped through her stimulating veins. The chambers of her heart collapsing as her heartstrings pinged and her body was flushed of life. Her ribcage shattering like a broken heart as her last hair molecule came to a halt like the life she was destined to live. However, her's was being displaced by a possessive soul ready to be sacrificed to the devil himself.

Natalie Weston (13)
Barnwell Middle School, Shephall Green

THE STREETS

Whilst I walked down the streets the sunlight faded and the sky quickly turned black. Pebbles bombarded my feet as streetlights blinded my eyes and flickered in the distance. The sudden sound of thunder deafened my ears as the cold winter air blistered my body.

Walking through these streets at night is a deathtrap. Suddenly a bang from the alley nearby. I thought nothing of it until a man pulled me in. With his face covered, I knew there was trouble.

My eyes closed. I slipped into unconsciousness. My soul left my body. He escaped, taking all my possessions.

Eddie Crawford (13)

Barnwell Middle School, Shephall Green

BLINK ONCE, BLINK TWICE

The man chased me growling like a rabid dog. He had vomited and defecated all at once with a blood tinted-looking vomit bubble. I looked at his eyes. He looked at me. He stared and gazed like he was intoxicated. His blue eyes stared into the darkness.

I blinked once in a lonely corridor. He just stared. I got up. I was against the wall feeling dead. I blinked again. He slowly started to mumble, "H...e...l...p m...e." I approached him and said, "Don't worry." He bit my leg. Now I'm like that man. Unable to speak. The virus controls me.

Jamie Bowe (12)
Barnwell Middle School, Shephall Green

YOU'RE NOT ALONE

What was that? Creaking floorboards... ticking clocks, broken windows. A strong smell was coming from the room next to me like something's rotting. My teeth were chattering, my fingers were shaking and I felt like I wasn't alone. Sort of like someone was watching my every move. Sometimes, I can hear a faint squeak of a door opening, but I think it's just my imagination. I hope. Panting fast, I slowly opened the door. I wasn't about to go downstairs. Trust me, I just have a feeling... I opened the door. 3, 2, 1... Grandma? She was covered in blood...

Abigail Burrell (12)
Barnwell Middle School, Shephall Green

THE MAN THROUGH THE WINDOW

I was once a little girl strolling through the woods with my mum, older brother, younger brother and older sister. I am ever so slightly behind them, and that is when I saw him. His face, concealed behind a black mask. I didn't think anything of this and carried on walking. A few moments later, I felt a cold, gloved hand cover my mouth and grab me from behind whilst pulling me backwards, my screams were muffled. I tried to fight back whilst yelling. "Help," but not a living single soul could hear me. I got deeper into the woods...

Aaliyah Holloway (12)
Barnwell Middle School, Shephall Green

WHAT WE DON'T SEE

I couldn't focus. This essay had to be the most boring piece of work ever. All I could think about was... Wait. What was that? Something moving, in the reflection of my computer screen? I could feel myself begin to sweat, my heart rapidly pounding. My head swivelled around. Nothing there. I was just paranoid. Then I felt it - something using all of its strength, tugging at my head. I tried to breathe, to scream, but I couldn't. Still, I couldn't see anything there, it was just pain. Then, before the end, I saw it. What we don't see.

Imogen Spiller (13)
Barnwell Middle School, Shephall Green

FULL MOON

The sirens were blaring, his hands shaking: they knew. He ran up the stairs and out of the house and with the knife dripping with blood he left his calling card ... a black rose. He went to his safe house. He sat there with a feeling of fulfilment, yet a desire for more. Who's he you ask? He's the Black Rose Killer. By dawn, it was all over the news, He was proud, what sociopathic serial killer wouldn't be? By now you're probably wondering why, well it started when he was fifteen just after his mother (Rose) was murdered...

Tanisha Chilton (12)
Barnwell Middle School, Shephall Green

MY FINAL DIARY!

My name's Katlyn and my day so far has been strange. I keep getting the feeling someone's watching and following me everywhere. I went to the shop earlier and I swear I saw someone in the corner of my eye, no one was there. It's four hours later and strange things keep happening, I keep hearing doors opening and closing. I keep asking if it's my mother coming home from work but no one answers. It's now late at night. I took a long nap to distract myself from reality, where is everyone? Why is no one home? I disappeared!

Ellie Kirby (13)
Barnwell Middle School, Shephall Green

THE CUBE OF IRIS

The scar on the doll shone in the moonlight. The blood-red knife was searching for a victim. *Splash!* The victim was spotted by Iris. They were unaware that the doll was stalking like a lion to a gazelle. The rain was getting heavier as the doll got closer. They spotted the two-foot Iris. The pace of the doll, rain and the person all sped up at once. The knife was thrown at force straight at the person's head, coming out the other side. The person's eye socket was blasted out of their face, blood washed away with the rain.

Kian Price (14)
Barnwell Middle School, Shephall Green

I SWEAR I HEARD THEM...

It was never my fault, all the things that happened to me. My mother never really paid attention to me, nor my sibling, that's probably why they died that night... in the car on the highway. I don't remember much, I was too young; I was told that my mother was drunk and I was lucky to survive. There is one thing though...They say my sibling died, but that's what doesn't sit right with me. I was young but I knew their voices, always so sweet like candy. Oh yeah, my name. Wait, was that, the door...? What...?

Isla Lowery (13)
Barnwell Middle School, Shephall Green

THE GRAVESTONE

It was a normal Friday night when a group of ten friends started to have a stroll down the street. They came across a graveyard and decided to explore it but they didn't know what they had started. After a few hours, most of them were drunk but they needed some of them to direct the group home. As they were leaving they knocked over a gravestone and the three people that weren't drunk tried to pick up the gravestone as the overs laughed. Then the tallest boy got dragged down and a shadow-like figure scooped his eyes out slowly.

Ethan Bartlett (12)
Barnwell Middle School, Shephall Green

SCHOOL LIFE

I thought we were all safe, a place where there is no harm, no horror but I was wrong... no one is safe! It was just another day at school with boring lessons and boring teachers, just another regular day... until a student slammed the door open with nothing but their body. The person had bite marks on her body top to bottom. She looked as if she was a walking corpse. She started biting everyone, killing them! That was the day I lost everything, my friends, my family, my teachers. The only thing keeping me happy was killing them!

Pyper Thomas (11)
Barnwell Middle School, Shephall Green

HELP ME

I moved into a new house. I walked in and felt a weird feeling, but I didn't think anything of it. I went to bed and woke up to my door opening slowly. I felt a cold hand grab me and drag me somewhere. I don't remember much. Someone or something took me to the red room that I have never seen before. It was pitch-black. Something whispered to me, "You will not escape, have fun." I've never screamed so loudly in my life. I started running towards the door, it slammed shut. "Help me!" I was silenced.

Kimberly Heath (12)
Barnwell Middle School, Shephall Green

GODZILLA

The day was 10th April 1954, a sea patrol was scouting for trouble in the area. So far there wasn't much until a large beam of blue shot from the sky. That was the last of the patrol.

Now it's the 8th April 2021, the city was normal until a large creature rose from the sea. Screams everywhere. The monster roared, wind blowing at speed. Then its back glowed. A large beam came out of its mouth, Tokyo was destroyed.

The city was a pit of fire. People lay dead, burnt. The monster roared. That was the end of Tokyo.

Alfie Horner (13)

Barnwell Middle School, Shephall Green

THE VOICE...

When I was seven years old, I shared a room with my siblings. Every night before we went to bed our mother would always tuck us in. We always knew there was something living in our house but our mother never believed us, but this night was different from the others... The creature who lived in our house seemed off, he seemed different...

Later that night, I got ready for bed. As I lay my head down on the pillow a soft whisper filled my ears. It said in such a small voice that I could barely hear. "Get out..."

Abigail Cross (12)
Barnwell Middle School, Shephall Green

HALLOWS EVE MURDERS

"Oh, how I adore Halloween." I didn't know this was my last. I knocked on the door with my sweet bucket. I smiled with excitement as I knocked on the door, waiting for a scare or a scream. I didn't notice that hands had grabbed onto my legs and arms, I was pulled in. I screamed for help and cried. I realised the hands had gone into the darkness and something was moving along my leg. I could get just a glimpse of a butcher's knife, which then cut straight through me. One was above my neck. It fell down.

Kai Jellis (12)
Barnwell Middle School, Shephall Green

THE CAVE HYBRIDS

I remember the day in that cave, it was full of blood-sucking vampires that turn into wolves, they call themselves hybrids. That day was frightening. I thought they were going to hurt me or my friends.

My friends and I are going camping and we're going to explore a cave. As soon as we got there we set up the tents and everything. "Sam, have you got some sticks to use later for the fire?"

It was finally time to go explore the cave. We ran there and as soon as we went in there was heavy breathing...

Hannah Hayhurst (12)

Barnwell Middle School, Shephall Green

THE DOORS TO HELL

Finally. There it was standing right in front of me. The tall dark brick walls peering down on me. I took a few steps closer down the cobble path, my heart getting faster each second. Dark clouds towered over me. I could see the giant double-door and started getting eager to turn the handle. Another side of me just wanted to turn back and go home, however, I ignored it. I was too desperate. I laid my hand on the dusty handle and the door creaked open slowly. I stepped inside and then all of a sudden, the floor crumbled.

Sienna-Star John (13)
Barnwell Middle School, Shephall Green

THE DOLLS

Bob and Jim were walking through an abandoned shopping mall on a chilly, dark day. They spotted a doll shop, the lights were on and it looked open as if you could go inside and buy something. The boys were drawn in by this... odd shop. The boys decided to go in. Inside the shop, there was no till and nobody inside. A creak was heard. It was behind them. The room fell silent again. In the corner of Bob's eye, he saw something move. Looking left, Bob didn't see Jim beside him and the shelves suddenly had no dolls.

Ross Green (14)
Barnwell Middle School, Shephall Green

THE NEW STUDENT

When I go to class, there's a new student. He is oddly pale with dark hair and peering at him I get a terrible feeling about him. After school, I see him head into the woods. I watch suspiciously and gasp as I see him shovelling handfuls of red meat into his mouth, blood running between his fingers. Then it hits me what's so off about him, he's a vampire. I spot a sharp-looking stick on the ground. I grab it, sneaking behind him, but he whips round, smirks at me and sinks his razor-sharp teeth into my neck.

Farran Rose (13)
Barnwell Middle School, Shephall Green

THE WOMAN, THE MIRROR

The sound was getting louder... With sweat dripping down my neck and my unsteady hands trembling I put my ear to the base of the door. I heard footsteps getting louder and louder. Suddenly the creaks of the wood stopped. I let out a sigh of relief as I stood up to get back to bed.

Later that night I woke up and turned my body over. Then out of the corner of my eye, I saw a woman in black rags and long black hair concealing her eyes standing, waiting, in my mirror watching me sleep. Waiting just waiting...

Olivia Jackson (12)
Barnwell Middle School, Shephall Green

THE WHITE WISH

One day, on a distant planet, an alien named Bobjim was praying with his family and he wished for someone to help him and make him understand where to go in life.
Later that night, Bobjim was very tired and trying to sleep. However, there was a storm brewing outside. All of a sudden, a lightning strike came straight through his window and hit beside his bed. Bobjim then saw a white figure standing over him. Bobjim was never seen again. Meanwhile, his funeral was held with no body for proof that he was dead.

Liam McGarry (12)
Barnwell Middle School, Shephall Green

EDWARD SANCHEZ

There was a man, an evil man, who did experiments on humans and animals to try and create aliens. He was named Edward Sanchez.

One day one of his experiments went wrong, a monstrous alien took him over. The evilness took control. He went to get revenge for his mother. His deadbeat dad lived not far away. He went to his house and brutally murdered his own father. He then attacked all the bullies at his primary school but was then arrested and executed but the evilness will come back, it always comes back.

Oliver Moss (13)

Barnwell Middle School, Shephall Green

SMILE DOG

On a stormy night, I was home alone with my hamsters running around with loads of energy and my two dogs lying on the sofa. Suddenly, my dogs started barking like crazy. I went to look at what they were barking at when my dogs pulled my trousers, trying to drag me back. When I turned around to tell them to stop there was nobody there. No dogs, no hamsters. I ran upstairs to look for them but what I saw horrified me. There was a dog-looking monster eating my hamsters with my dogs ripped apart. I ran...

Jobe Orphanou (12)
Barnwell Middle School, Shephall Green

IT FOUND ME

I turned the corner and held my breath. It was there. I glanced around and noticed a broken, rusty torch in a pile of rubble. I rushed over and pointed the shiny beam at the ghost. It disappeared. I stumbled and hurried to get away before it found me again and something happened. Suddenly, I felt something. A cold hand was placed on my back. I froze. It was here, it found me. I held my breath and wanted the ground to open up and eat me as it slowly walked around me. There we were. Face to face.

Amelia Ingram-Tedd (12)
Barnwell Middle School, Shephall Green

SMILE DOG

One night I was home alone with my cat on the couch watching Netflix, when my cat suddenly turned to the window. Raindrops slowly dripped down it. I saw nothing so I turned away and as I did I heard a scratch on the window, I jumped up and there I saw the thing that I have heard rumours of, Smile Dog... It stared at me nefariously. In a blink of an eye, it disappeared. In the distance, I could hear scratches, then I felt one on my leg... It wasn't my cat because I got her nails clipped...

Nashvil Coutinho (13)
Barnwell Middle School, Shephall Green

WHAT DID I DO?

The vibration of the whistles made me scared. They were haunting and vicious, like the sound of wolves. Could it be wolves or something else? I saw a figure upstairs. The windows banged open. I cried. I saw something coming towards me. Could this be the end? I felt a sudden breeze to my leg. I felt something grab me and it pulled me away. Only God could see the threats of this creature. Then I saw it, a person floating in the air. What was it and what have I done to deserve it? What did I do?

Meso Onyeukwu (12)
Barnwell Middle School, Shephall Green

HIM

I still remember the pain, the feeling when I found out I had been betrayed by him, the only one I trusted. I remember the cool steel knife in my hand, the adrenaline coursing through my body as I walked up to him. I remember him falling to his knees, body trembling as he begged me for mercy. I remember the crimson blood dripping onto my hands as the life drained out of his petrified eyes. I poured the gasoline and walked away, a smirk spreading across my face. I don't regret a thing.

Ashleigh Hudspith (13)
Barnwell Middle School, Shephall Green

THE LADY AT THE END OF THE BED

I moved into a new house. When I arrived, all I got was chills and a sick feeling in my stomach. The first few nights in the house, my dog was constantly barking at the corner of the room, it was very loud. I took no notice of it until one night, I was in bed and I felt my bed aggressively shaking. There was a lady standing at the end of my bed. "Get out of my house," she screamed. This made me so scared I was put into a coma. This happened six years ago, I'm still scared.

Hollie Hickman (13)
Barnwell Middle School, Shephall Green

THE GIRL NEXT DOOR

There was a girl named Jessica, she was always in the corner of the classroom. Nobody really knew what she was doing with her life until the day of her disappearance. She was found in the lake next to the forest. There were many rumours which spread around. 'It was suicide' or 'she probably fell in the river'. That one was a very popular thought, however, nobody really knows. Only two people know the truth. However, I couldn't let anyone know the truth.

Kenan Catchpole-Mateu (12)
Barnwell Middle School, Shephall Green

THE MIST

The mist, a cloud of mystery engulfs whatever it crosses and disappears. Bringing blindness wherever it goes. A pale white mist is all it is or so it may seem at first. A creature lurking, waiting and wanting. Like the sin of greed waiting, wanting and teetering on the edge of humanity. Towns left torn from the ground and stained blood-red in its wake.
"I feed, I hunger, for I am the mist and I am wanting more, more, more."
Are you next...?

Ramero Shepherd (13)
Barnwell Middle School, Shephall Green

THE WOODS

The wind was howling through the trees as the moon dominated the night sky looking like a black hole, everything crossing vanishes without a trace. Ben ran as fast as he could, leaving the hungry wolf behind him with dust in his eyes. He was able to make it inside the ancient house creaking with every step he took without being made the wolf's dinner...

Kieran Wyatt (13)
Barnwell Middle School, Shephall Green

I THINK SHE LIKED IT A BIT TOO MUCH...

She had never done this before. It wasn't a normal thing for her. I think she liked it a bit too much. The feeling of the warm blood over her hands, watching it puncture through his soft skin, with a laugh so creepy yet innocent at the same time. I don't know why she did this, I thought she loved me but apparently not.
I will be back... I promise.

Olivia Kirkhoff (11)
Barnwell Middle School, Shephall Green

HOTEL

It was Friday the 13th July 2009. Bobba and Ross were flying
to Mexico the next day from Gatwick Airport. They were on
the way to the hotel to stay as the airport is three hours
away. They arrived at the hotel at 8pm. Once checked in
they entered their hotel and were greeted by horror. A
woman was dying with a big sword in her.

Max Allen (14)
Barnwell Middle School, Shephall Green

THE FIRE

It was burnt, reduced to ashes. People say it's haunted, I don't believe that. Staring at it, ominous winds push past, the sky goes grey but that doesn't scare me. Going in alone, it sounds like I can hear whispers. "Is that Gabe? Can't be, he died in the fire..."

Freddy Chapman (15)
Barnwell Middle School, Shephall Green

POLICE COVER-UP

I didn't mean to kill her. Twelve hours later... "A sixteen-year-old girl, found dead, in an abandoned alleyway, shot dead in the chest. She was last seen alive, with her friend after school, doing cheerleading. She was wearing her blue and yellow cheerleading uniform. That wasn't the unusual thing about the murder, her friends said she got changed into her gym clothes: she was last seen wearing her black Nike Pro shorts and her plain black top with a lace back. If anyone has seen these clothes anywhere they shouldn't have been, please contact 111."

Shanira Hardy (13)
Barnwell School Upper School, Stevenage

SHADOWS

Cold shadows pierce the eyes of the deceiver, they manipulate the receiver. Icy black fills the room. Always sleep with one eye open, you never know what's out in the open. Harsh footsteps scold your mind, the sky looking down in disappointment. The wind sways the atmosphere as the grey mist covers what was once a beautiful blue sky. They form a dark, brooding face, a face she has never seen of that sort of shape. Razor-sharp cheekbones, slender nose, narrow frame. Run from this madness, run from the danger, fear, blood, sweat and tears. It's all or nothing.

Hanifa Ashraf (14)
Barnwell School Upper School, Stevenage

FRIEND NOT KILLER

Why? She said it needed to be done to survive but she's gone. I shouldn't have helped her but it's too late now, I must run. It's coming closer and there's a dead end. We chose the forest so no one would see us but now it's just a trap that I cannot escape. Why does she run from me? All my life I have been lonely. Dad did try and kill me in an experiment but only successfully shredded half my face and gave me claws for a hand. She sacrificed the girl to be my friend. Didn't she?

Anisa Ashraf (14)
Barnwell School Upper School, Stevenage

A SUDDEN STORY

The door lay shut for 200 years. Nobody dared to open it because the last person who opened it went missing for four years and two months. When they came back, they were dead. Nobody knew how the person died or managed to come there himself. It is a mystery that the public is counting on me to find out. So I opened the door, bravely and I died. The sight of darkness chilled me to the bone. I felt like a feather as I was lifted off the ground. The sky was my next and final destination.

Tiffany Nell (11)
Benedict Biscop CE Academy, Moorside

STAIRWAY TO OBLIVION

The door abruptly opens, releasing the shriek from its insides. My feet take me in. Emptiness. Faded crimson stains, highlighted against a backdrop of beige linoleum. Something drips casually from the ceiling, falling on my pallid cheek, like tears of resignation. My legs take my powerless body upstairs, creaking, mocking every step. A figure greets me, its slit-mouth opens wide, ready to receive its next victim. Blood-stained teeth and hands reach greedily forward. I refuse its ghoulish invitation, running fast past the creature. Trapped, cornered, I hear its deadly footsteps behind me. My efforts are futile, who am I kidding?

Ellora Chatwin (12)
Birkenhead School, Oxton

THE TALE OF THE TWISTED TOWN

"Let's go have a look," whispered Jane.

"I'm not sure," Christian cautioned.

"Don't be such a scaredy-cat."

They were standing in front of a village. Suddenly, a wailing noise came from one of the houses."Someone's in pain we have to help them," said Jane. Jane sprinted towards the village with Christian following her closely. When Jane reached the dilapidated house, she slowly opened the door and screamed. Suddenly, she was grabbed and pulled inside.

"Jane, where are you?" Christian called, concerned. Christian opened the door and found Jane locked in shackles. Turning quickly, Christian ran out and left Jane there.

Samuel Martin (12)
Bishopston Comprehensive School, Bishopston

THE OLD HOUSE

"Halt, Ava! You know it's off-limits," said Phoebe.

"I know," Ava replied. Her hands were trembling as she slid the lock open which protected the secret. Towering shadows formed around her; her heart raced as footsteps surrounded her.

Ava saw an old house. *I'll wait there and call Sasha,* she thought. She shivered. She crept between crumbling gravestones, heading for the house. She entered and shut the door behind me. "Hello?" No answer.

She called Sasha.

"I'll be there in ten, Millie!" she said. Ava sat on a dusty floor.

Bang! "Sasha?" A comforting hand touched her shoulder. "Sasha?"

Sophie Mather (13)
Bishopston Comprehensive School, Bishopston

LITTLE RED RIDING HOOD

"What great big ears you have!" said Little Red Riding Hood.
"Only to hear you with," said the wolf.
"What great big eyes you have!" said Little Red Riding Hood.
"Only to see you with," said the wolf.
"Where's Grandma?" said Little Red Riding Hood.
The wolf replied, "She's just sleeping, don't worry."
Little Red Riding Hood looked everywhere for her grandma and when she finally met the wolf again in the living room the wolf whispered, "Finally my dinner is here!" And all of a sudden Little Red Riding hood was gone. All that was left were her clothes.

Harriet Fox (12)
Bishopston Comprehensive School, Bishopston

THE HUMAN WALL

She moved into a house with her husband. Her husband's job was painting the upstairs. Her job was peeling off the wallpaper because for some reason the last owner wallpapered every wall of the house.

She started peeling wallpaper. She found a game to find which piece is biggest like when you peel dry skin after sunburn. When she peeled each wall she found a name and a date under the paper. She researched all these people online. These people were missing. The police arrived. She heard one policeman say, "It's human."

"What's human?"

"What you were peeling wasn't wallpaper!"

Anna Martin (12)
Bishopston Comprehensive School, Bishopston

THE GHOST OF US

We're alive but barely. "It's still following us," Mara whispered. We broke into a sprint, our knees bleeding and numb from the brambles painted with our blood.
A bloodcurdling screech emerged from the ancient woods.
"What a great idea Mara," I hissed. Mara was always fascinated by myths and when she heard about a 'ghost-ridden wood' she just had to go.
After what seems like hours of running we stop and set up camp. Our fire burning ferociously, we both sit in silence. We were so entranced by the flames we didn't notice a twig-like bony hand around Mara's neck.

Manon Lythgoe (11)
Bishopston Comprehensive School, Bishopston

THE UNKNOWN GHOST

The sunlight was creeping in. I knew I wouldn't make it back before morning. There was an old house in the distance. *I will wait there and call Liv,* I thought. Sunlight weaved around the house. I crept between the crumbling bricks, getting near to the house. The door was missing, but there was a corridor. I entered. "Hello?" No answer. I called Liv. "I will be there in five," she said as I sat on a dusty chair. Broken windows, empty rooms and odd furniture. *Bang!* "Liv?" The shadow getting bigger and bigger. A soft hand touched me. "Liv?"

Emily Taylor (13)
Bishopston Comprehensive School, Bishopston

KILLER IN THE HOUSE

It was the last day of summer. Alex invited her friends around for a sleepover, including her best friends Cedric, Lilly and Brad. Alex lived on the other side of town in a grand mid-century house with gothic features. Excited, they all entered through the heavy wooden door, ignoring the dark shadows that seemed to loom in the upstairs window. Alex greeted them and her parents seemed nice enough. *What could go wrong?* they all thought. After playing on Alex's PlayStation 5, it was dinner. They said, "Cheers," and drank, however, suddenly the room went dark. They screamed in panic.

Daniel Adams (15)
Bishopston Comprehensive School, Bishopston

THE ENDLESS FOREST

In the middle of an endless forest, there lies a desolate house decorated with destroyed windows and wallpaper desperately peeling off, like it knows the hazard for staying inside the barbed wire prison. Fog clouds the floor like it's holding on for dear life, hoping for a sign of escape, wind howls in warning, however, if you were to listen carefully you would hear the lingering of steps treading on leaves, for some love adventure and become deaf to the signs of dread.

"C'mon Ava, let's go back." A whisper, but still heard. Unfortunately, they have already gone too far...

Hollie Davies (12)
Bishopston Comprehensive School, Bishopston

WHY DID SHE TRUST HER?

It was a cold, dark night, no noise, no movement, no signs of life. The night sky was as black as coal with stars shining like torches. Libby and Emma decided to go on a walk that cold and silent night, but little did they know that everything could change in just a split second.

Just as the girls approached the abandoned, dilapidated-looking house, Emma turned to Libby and whispered, "Libby, is this a good idea?"

"Yes, of course, it is, why wouldn't it be?" Libby responded.

Ever since then Emma's family have always thought, *why did she trust her?*

Liv Thomas (12)
Bishopston Comprehensive School, Bishopston

THE DREAM

A dark, stormy night in the depths of the gloomy woods. The silence was broken by the sound of leaves crunching under the girl's feet, the thunder crackling, scaring the birds and the wind howling, making the leaves spin into the thundery dark sky. The girl's pace started getting faster, the crackling of the leaves becoming more frequent until, silence.
No more sound was heard, no more footsteps of the girl's feet. Out of nowhere, a figure in black appeared approaching the girl. He laughed. And then, "Honey! Wake up!" To the girl's shock, it was a dream all along...

Sienna Warren (12)
Bishopston Comprehensive School, Bishopston

THE WORST FLIGHT OF MY LIFE

In the dead of night, six hours into my flight, I woke in fright. The sound system turned on and the captain said with a trembling voice, "We're going down, prepare for landing!" "With nothing in sight, where we will land?" I asked myself. The captain said, "Here is a small fact: You're are going to die." My mouth dropped. Was he joking? I was plummeting downwards. Vibrations rippled through me as the water broke, glass shattering everywhere, water gushing into the plane. There was no way I was getting out of here alive. I never saw light again.

Evie Manning (13) & Poppy Harry-Thomas
Bishopston Comprehensive School, Bishopston

THERE'S SOMETHING IN THE FOREST

One frosty day there was a girl, she lived in a small village. The adults always said, "Don't go outside the village wall," but she didn't listen. Every day she sneaked outside the village.

She was outside the village when she heard singing, "Who's there?" she asked terrified, but there was no response. She followed the singing into the forest, but suddenly the singing stopped. She saw a shadow emerge and chase her to its den where she was never seen again. Some say if you go to the forest the day she disappeared you can still hear her singing.

Tehillah Thomas (12)
Bishopston Comprehensive School, Bishopston

A CURIOUS WARNING!

I was sitting in my living room last night, watching TV, when I heard an astonishing sound. It was a scraping noise over the hardwood floor. I was perplexed, I looked for the source. A folded note had been pushed under the door. I approached the note nonchalantly, more intrigued than anything else. My heart pounded like a war drum!
I knelt down gingerly and took the paper in my hands. Words were scrawled on it, 'Get out of here. He's coming!' I didn't wait to contemplate the note's meaning. Something was seriously wrong. The message was exuding blood!

Phoebe Holt (14)
Bishopston Comprehensive School, Bishopston

THE ABANDONED POLICE STATION

Early one evening, a police chief and a captain went on patrol. They got a call about shots fired outside an abandoned police station. The shooter was killed by police officers. After the shooter's body was removed, the chief and captain saw the abandoned police station. Trembling, they went inside the abandoned police station and they found a bunch of bodies. The captain fainted in shock and the chief gave the captain first aid. The captain woke up. Shaking and screaming, they started to run out of the station. A figure loomed in the shadows and started to follow them...

Ioan Marvelley (13)
Bishopston Comprehensive School, Bishopston

THE GHOST OF ALBERT VON FIZZLE

"On a night just like tonight, a ghost was seen roaming castle ruins finding victims to kill! Some say it is the ghost of scientist Albert Von Fizzle and he's come to get revenge!" said Alice. Just then a breeze blew through the woods and the faint sound of footsteps could be heard coming closer and closer.

Suddenly a pair of floating blue eyes appeared and said, "I am the ghost of Albert Von Fizzle, I have come to get revenge!"

They all screamed and ran out. "Well they did want a scare!" said Banshee appearing from behind a tree.

Chloe Marfell (11)
Bishopston Comprehensive School, Bishopston

ABANDONED HAUNTED SCHOOL

Late one evening, strange noises came from the abandoned, haunted school on the hill. Nessa went to go investigate and Tristan came to help her. As they tiptoed through the rotting, damp school, something flew through the cracked window. Suddenly, they saw a small girl in the school hallway, crying. As they went to go check on her, suddenly she started floating. They realised she wasn't any normal girl, she was a possessed ghost! Running to the other side of the dark and scary hallway, they thought they'd got away until they saw red eyes peering from the darkness...

Tristan Crocker (14)
Bishopston Comprehensive School, Bishopston

A DARK NIGHT IN

It was May 2nd 2008. At Veron Avenue, Number 527, a pair of seven year olds were playing in the streets, pacing round, shouting with joy, everything perfect. Or so they thought. As the day drew closer to an end, the stars appeared and the boys heard a strange howling noise. Being curious boys, they went to explore, but as they peered around a prickly bush they discovered the dead body of their maths teacher! "Yaaaaaaaayyy!" they both yelled. "No more maths!" The killer wasn't satisfied so went to the noise as well and they were never seen again.

Albert Mattingly (13)
Bishopston Comprehensive School, Bishopston

MIND GAMES

Darkness descends on the forest. I creep forward, *why did I have to wander off?* Something rushes past me, *a gust of wind?* Leaves rustle ahead as I feel the overwhelming urge to walk towards it. *What am I doing?* The twisted trees seemed to whisper, telling me to leave. But I couldn't. *This is a bad idea.* My legs pulled me forward. I saw a bright beaming light flickering. I reached to touch it but my head snapped round as a bloodcurdling scream echoed around me.
I wake up in a hospital, it hits me. The scream was me...

Sasha Turner (13) & Martha
Bishopston Comprehensive School, Bishopston

HORROR AT THE TRAIN STATION

The sun had set and the moon was bright but the sky was dark and gloomy. I'd just arrived at the train station when a large cloud of fog surrounded me. I couldn't see anything; the lights flickered on and off. Suddenly, I saw a large black figure standing in the distance. I turned the other way when the lights flickered again, I felt a hand brush across my face, shivers rushed through my body. The strange mysterious figure came closer and closer. I saw blood-red eyes staring at me directly. Everything went black. Something pulled me onto the train...

Millie Bray (13)
Bishopston Comprehensive School, Bishopston

THE LASTING GUN

The wind blew hard. The rain crashed down. The tree's bark hung by a piece of moss, as if thread, getting battered by the gloomy night. The ants scattered across the drowning path, struggling for air, attempting to pass. The lonely ghost watched the once a year depressing season come round again and again. For the ghost was a former hunter murdered by a fox for his troublesome horrific acts and has remained lonely in the wood for eternity. No love. No one. The foxes watched him rot away. Then... *Bang...* Who said he didn't have his gun still?

Evie Basher (12) & Charlotte
Bishopston Comprehensive School, Bishopston

THE GHOST OF THE HAUNTED MANSION

Once upon a time, there was a mansion in the middle of a wood on the outskirts of a village. It had been deserted for nearly a decade. "Argh!" Another scream from the mansion. This happened every night.

One night Harry was out with his friends playing manhunt. Harry ran far from his friend Joe who was 'it'. Then suddenly there was a screech from ahead. He froze. He had run all the way to the mansion. Ghosts started pouring out of the windows and headed for Harry. He was dead in seconds. That's why nobody goes to the woods.

Laurie Messam (12)
Bishopston Comprehensive School, Bishopston

HAUNTED SCHOOL

Late at night, there were two teens, one girl and one boy exploring an old haunted school. The wind battered against the windows and groans and creaks echoed around the classroom. "What was that?" Emma said freaking out. So they did the one thing they knew how to do: they ran away. But, before Emma could, someone or something grabbed her arm and pulled her away. Ben tried to grab her arm but missed because he tripped over something on the ground. The last thing he heard was Emma's piercing scream as she was dragged away into the darkness.

Molly Howard (13)
Bishopston Comprehensive School, Bishopston

THE GHOST OF THE MANSION

Once upon a time, there was a mansion in the creepy woods called Hollow Howl. Nobody had ever lived there except an old man who died a couple of days ago. Tourists walking past have said they've seen white figures in the smashed windows of the mansion. Nobody dared to go near it. However, one day a 15-year-old boy decided to explore the abandoned mansion. The boy approached the dilapidated mansion and opened the front door. Inside, there was broken glass all over the floor. He turned around and was shocked. There it was... the ghost of the mansion.

Tyler Davies (12)
Bishopston Comprehensive School, Bishopston

THE CHOICE

There were two close friends. They were at a park when the sun started going down. One said, "It's getting late, let's go home."
The other said, "Okay but let me go to the restroom first." After he left he started walking home to his house. Then he got a call from her mum asking where she was. He replied, "I was with her at the park. I don't know where she is." The mother started getting worried and ended the call. He stood there confused and still wondering why he had chosen to kill her in the restroom.

Seren Jones (11)
Bishopston Comprehensive School, Bishopston

HAUNTED MOTEL

Early one evening, an explorer, John, visited one of the most haunted motels in the country. As he entered, he felt immediately uncomfortable, as if someone was watching him. John tentatively climbed the creaky stairs when all of a sudden there was a crash and he fell into the basement. He saw a dark figure in the corner, despite his fear, he kept exploring. The room was old and spooky with a battered cabinet in the corner. Slowly, he opened it and there was a sudden rush towards him. A ghostly spectre reached out and pulled him into the darkness.

Etienne Pinto (13)
Bishopston Comprehensive School, Bishopston

APOCALYPSE

"Bye Jim," said Thomas as he left the park. "See you tomorrow!" It was getting dark so I decided to call Mum to pick me up. Suddenly thick fog rolled over the park, I saw shadows lurking on the grass. This was getting too scary so I dialled Mum's number as quick as I could.

"Hi Jim, are you alright?" she said as she answered the phone. *No answer.* I heard whispers all around and all of a sudden I froze. My phone dropped to the floor with a thud and I was swiftly dragged away by some unknown creature.

Toby Hulatt (13)

Bishopston Comprehensive School, Bishopston

THE BLACK HAT

There was once a girl who accidentally strolled into the woods. She was petrified and shocked by the screeches of the owls and howls of the wolves. She came across a black hat. She gently tapped the hat so it fell over, and there was a white note that said, 'Whoever shall wear this hat, will experience pain, horror and misery for the rest of their days'. She laughed and mumbled, "Sure it will." She then picked up the hat and put it on. She felt strange and weird, not knowing what happened. She realised, her skin was inside out.

Jack Arnold (12)
Bishopston Comprehensive School, Bishopston

A DARK NIGHT IN

On May 4th two men named Phil and Jessie were having a couple of drinks at Phil's gorgeous flat. Jessie left tired in his car but then as Phil closed the door he heard a bang at his door. Phil said to himself, "Jessie must have forgotten something." But the sparkling stars had turned into clouds, the rain started falling and there was no Jessie. He heard a bang at his bedroom door. Slowly and cautiously Phil went up to his bedroom door. He gently opened it. "Argh!" From that moment on there was no sign of Phil or Jessie.

Sonny Curtis (13)
Bishopston Comprehensive School, Bishopston

SILENT SCREAMS

The silent screams are the worst ones, the ones that curdle your tears. Last night will go down in history for Molly Blake's deafening squeals, The killer prepared his knife last night while waiting under the bed. The knife's purpose? To end a life; to end a childhood; to end a generation. He made sure to make it slow and painful so he could watch the pain sink into her eyes and the light get dragged away. This silent scream burst through the roof, through walls, the windows and all. Molly drew her last breath, never to be seen again...

Amelia Griffiths (13) & Eden
Bishopston Comprehensive School, Bishopston

THE GIRL OF THE LAKE

Ellina woke up startled, sweat dripping down her face, her hair plastered to her forehead. She heard it. The scream ringing in her ears. She swung her feet out of her bed. She fumbled for the candle, the flame dancing on the wick. She cautiously dragged her feet towards the door which creaked as she opened it. Slowly, she walked out of the house as if under a curse, her feet dragging in the mud. Ellina waded into the lake. Suddenly, she stopped. Fear boiling in her blood, she ran but couldn't, she was being pulled vigorously into the lake.

Anna Williams (13)
Bishopston Comprehensive School, Bishopston

BEYOND THE FOG

I stared into the fog waiting for her to return. I waited there for what seemed like hours before finally deciding to venture in myself. I walked through the eerie, abandoned, desolate town not seeing my hand before my face. *Crash!* Something fell behind me. I dared to look and shivers ran down my spine. I turned again. The feeling of the devil's eyes stared through to my soul. I saw my German Shepherd lunging towards me but I could see right through her. She leapt into me. My heart stopped. I went cold. I was with her once again.

Emily Brown (13) & Lara Edwards
Bishopston Comprehensive School, Bishopston

THE HAUNTED MANSION

I was having a walk one night when I came across this old, disgusting, filthy, scary mansion. I decided to investigate. I opened the door and it was dark and spooky!
Luckily, I brought a torch and I switched it on. What I saw was bodies decaying, walls crumbling and blood dripping down from the ceiling! I was horrified by all of this!
Suddenly, the torch batteries died. Then all of a sudden I heard something coming. Then out of nowhere a giant, gruesome beast jumped out in front of me!
I ran away screaming and I never looked back!

Lucca Benjamin Smith (14)

Bishopston Comprehensive School, Bishopston

BEHIND THE MIST

The mist was creeping in. I decided it was my turn. I felt a shooting shiver down my spine. My teeth clattered together! "Stop, Mike!" exclaimed my father with fear in his eyes.
I was fearful but I had already begun edging toward the cold stone door which led to the mist.
My hands were trembling as I slid the tight lock open which protected us from the secret I was about to unfold. Before I had the chance to take a step forward I couldn't see further than my own hand, but suddenly I heard a deafening shriek...

Eres Parry (13)
Bishopston Comprehensive School, Bishopston

COTTAGE GROVE'S END

On June 15th a small town in Minnesota was about to experience a storm like no other. Kids went to school, and adults went to work as usual before the tornado. The storm started at 19:27 and would last until the morning of the 18th. The residents of Cottage Grove shut their windows and prepared to stay inside. First came the tornado and then the deafening thunder, then silence. The Grange Family emerged on the 18th from their house only to find the whole town had vanished leaving only the wreckage of what once was Cottage Grove.

Esther Harman-Cashmore (12)
Bishopston Comprehensive School, Bishopston

THE TEXT

12/6/2020
(New Message)
Unknown: Hey number neighbour.
You: Hey.
Unknown: What are you up to?
You: Nothing much.
Unkown: Same here.
Unknown: Not much you can do with everything.
You: I suppose not.
Unknown: Where are you from?
You: I'm not going to tell you that.
Unknown: Oh come on, don't be such a tease!
You: I have to go now.
Unknown: No you don't.
You: Yes I do!
Unknown: Can you at least tell me your name?
You: Why do you need to know that?
Unknown: Because I want to know who I'm looking at.

Jake Cowell (13)
Bishopston Comprehensive School, Bishopston

A DEMON IN DISGUISE

They'd just come back from a car boot sale and Lucy was hugging the doll she'd bought. She said she was going to bed and hopped up the stairs. She was so excited for her first night with her new toy. Lucy placed the doll on the floor. Peacefully, she closed her eyes and drifted off. Later that night she was awoken by a groaning noise, assumed it was nothing but heard it again. Suddenly, the doll moved. Lucy lay as still as possible until the doll screeched. A ghostly figure arose from the doll and flew around the room.

Phoebe Jago (12)
Bishopston Comprehensive School, Bishopston

FOGGY FOREST

Exploring the forest seemed a good idea in the daylight. And then all of a sudden there was a loud shrieking scream. I started creeping around the dark stormy forest. Fog was creeping in and the sun was setting. I wandered around and I saw a dark, old, creepy house. Walking past the house, I heard voices and decided to investigate. I took a step forward to see that the door opened. I stumbled around lost and confused to see a little girl in an old, muddy dress. I immediately thought that must have been the girl that screamed.

Mali Gregory (12)
Bishopston Comprehensive School, Bishopston

DAD?

I got home just as the black blanket of fog surrounded the sky. I nestled beside the roaring fire while Dad calmly walked into the kitchen. Without warning a gunshot pierced my ears coming from the kitchen. Trembling, I sprinted into my room. I could feel my heart pounding against my chest all the while looking out the keyhole. Finally, my dad came upstairs and told me to unlock the door because it was safe. He just stared at me with his piercing blue eyes, but that didn't change the fact that my dad's eyes are green.

Leyah Nicholls (12)
Bishopston Comprehensive School, Bishopston

THE GHOSTS IN THE LIGHTHOUSE

Back in 1936, there was a lighthouse keeper and a scary lighthouse that everyone swore was haunted. There have been so many tales about this lighthouse, like how people have gone insane the second they opened the door. But this man wasn't afraid as he was a real lighthouse keeper. But then one day he saw something in the corner of his eye; he was old so he thought it was just his imagination and thought nothing of it. This kept happening and one day he saw them... the ghosts and souls of the dead pirates who had died.

Megan Richards (11)
Bishopston Comprehensive School, Bishopston

THE ABANDONED HOUSE

The storm was getting closer. I had no idea where I was. After miles of walking through the dark forest, I came to an abandoned house. I decided to go in for a while for some shelter from the pouring rain. My dog, Jimmy, suddenly started barking and ran straight up the spiral staircase in the centre of the room. I tried to chase him but he was too fast. I suddenly heard a scream coming from upstairs. I ran straight back out the door, across the graveyard without Jimmy. Soon after Jimmy came running out with a skull...

Libby Hale (12)
Bishopston Comprehensive School, Bishopston

ETERNAL DEATH

Nancy awoke on her birthday, she got ready and enjoyed the day. On her way home, she walked past a man, he had no face, flesh was pouring out of his skull. He stabbed her. She soon awoke; it was her birthday again. Was it a dream? She tries a different route home but the no-faced man shoots her outside. This happens for weeks until one day she decides to just not go to school. While she was asleep, the no-faced man dragged her through her window. People heard screams on the beach that night. She was never seen again.

Molly Jones (12)
Bishopston Comprehensive School, Bishopston

THE CAVE

I emerged from the suffocating darkness of the forest; there was nobody to be seen. My heart dropped as a blinding fog began to roll in. I saw a little ivy-ridden cave. I thought, *I have no choice, I will freeze out here.* I reluctantly stumbled toward the endless abyss that was the hungry mouth of the cave. Every noise I made echoed around me. As I sat on a rock, I saw something move in the corner of my eye. There was a flash of lightning, a shadow was cast on the wall of the cave. It wasn't human...

Luke Norman (13)
Bishopston Comprehensive School, Bishopston

BEHIND CLOSED DOORS

I didn't mean to kill her, until yesterday. As I was walking home I found a house, the only one on the street, but then I started to hear music to a lullaby! Suddenly, it made this ominous sound and then a girl walked out and dragged me in. She looked like a bloodied doll! Until I saw her face. She looked just like my friend who died yesterday. And then it happened. I remembered that I was walking on all the dead bodies including yours in this house and that I am the deadliest person behind you in school!

Samuel Eadon-Crosby (12)
Bishopston Comprehensive School, Bishopston

THE WICKED TRUTH OF THE SOUL TAKER

Long ago lived a sweet woman, but she was vicious. She was known back in the 50s as a kidnapper and a witch. Nobody chose to bother her as they'd be afraid of her taking their beloved children. She didn't do it just for fun, but because she wanted dinner. She has kids of her own that nobody has seen; she took her kid's life in her hands and used them for her own good. But when they reach an age she takes their soul, steals the life out of them then takes their lifeless body down to her basement.

Livvy Brereton (12)
Bishopston Comprehensive School, Bishopston

THE DARK SHADOW

In the cold misty night, there was a haunted house where all the glass was smashed, the floor was hollow, the ceiling and stairs were rotten. Cautiously, I tiptoed up the stairs. As I got to the top, laughing started at the end of the house and there were bats coming out of the room. A dark shadow flew past. My heart raced nervously as I got into the room. There was no one but shadows and creepy dolls on the floor. I slowly opened the wardrobe and a dark shadow jumped out on me. Death went through my mind.

Reuben Cain (14)
Bishopston Comprehensive School, Bishopston

INSANIUM

I awoke. There was a light shining in my face, I squinted and could make out a figure in the far corner of the room I had somehow awoken in. "Hello," he said, "are you feeling okay?" I tried speaking but then realised my lips had been stitched together. I started to panic as the man came closer to me, I tried getting up, but fell to the ground, as he had removed my kneecaps. I screamed, no sound, I forgot that my lips were sewn together. I gave up, and as I did the man left me to die.

James Hornsby-Smith (13)
Bishopston Comprehensive School, Bishopston

JACK AND THE BEANSTALK

Long ago there was a boy called Jack who grew a beanstalk that reached into the clouds. He climbed it and when he got to the top he saw a giant staring down at him. Suddenly the giant pulled the beanstalk out of the ground and ate it. Then a large chicken flew over to the giant, as soon as the chicken saw Jack it started sneezing because it was allergic to Jack. When the giant realised this, they threw Jack in their soup and ate him. The chicken and giant had a party and ate cheesy beans to celebrate.

Fern Thompson (12)
Bishopston Comprehensive School, Bishopston

A WEIRD DREAM

I was following someone, then chasing and then I was dead. Then I woke up. It had been but a weird dream. I went downstairs before I remembered I lived in a flat. As soon as I thought that I felt pain. I woke up. It had been a weird dream. I was in a car crash; my neck was broken. I woke up again. I was being stabbed then shot, then I woke up. My mum was there. She said, "Which one was your favourite?" The heading on the TV later... "Boy killed. How: unknown." My picture was there.

Harry Lewis (12)
Bishopston Comprehensive School, Bishopston

LIGHTS

It was 1am. Everything seemed silent. The lights were glaring into my soul. It would be a good idea to sleep as I had to wake up at 8am. I dragged myself to turn all of the lights off and wandered up the stairs. I reached the top with an odd feeling in my stomach; something was off. I spun around to see something in the darkness. My adrenaline was soaring at this point. What was it? I sprinted down the stairs faster than I ever had before to turn the light on again to find... my pet dog.

Charlotte Brady (13)
Bishopston Comprehensive School, Bishopston

DARKNESS

I heard a creak in the floorboards, it was pitch-black and silent outside. My stomach turned. Goosebumps were crawling along my body. I stayed under my duvet, deserted in darkness. I needed hydration but it was only coming out of my cold sweat. My door started to open, my heart was pounding. I heard footsteps coming towards me. I peeped my eyes over my duvet, I saw nothing but darkness. I felt a pain in my foot, it felt like someone was injecting me. My eyes started to open...

Aedan Mackenzie (14)
Bishopston Comprehensive School, Bishopston

MOUNTAIN MANIAC

Have you heard about the mountain maniac? Well, here's the start of my story... It all started earlier this morning. I was looking for fossils when someone who wasn't me was lurking around my patch. It was a dark figure, colossal but hunched over, deep royal blue eyes, sharp razor teeth which looked thirsty for fresh blood just like vampires. Snow covered its furry back, toes curled over, ears so small it was unusual. This creature was something I've never seen before, mysterious. Now I know I'm not alone. What else could be lurking through the shadows? The mountain maniac.

Poppy Tyson (13)
Chetwynde School, Barrow-In-Furness

SHROUDED HUNGER

I walked through my school gate, people happily talking around me. Suddenly, hunger started to envelop me. I tried ignoring my growing hunger, but it didn't stop. I took a step. My mouth started watering. Another step. I started to sweat profusely. The pain in my stomach, unbearable, I fell down, clutching my stomach. People started to stare, disgusted. I started coughing furiously. I closed my eyes, bit my hand, trying to calm my endless hunger. Thankfully, the temporary solution worked for now. My hand was bleeding. My teary eyes opened again. What a great start to the school day.

Nathan Lee Cheong (13)
Chetwynde School, Barrow-In-Furness

KOINONIPHOBIA

I'm in an ominous room, I've been here approximately thirty minutes just sitting down waiting for someone to help. I'm starting to think I'm stuck here. I don't even remember how I got here or what happened today. I guess I'm gonna have to start walking to the door. *You think you're going to have a bad time.* Once I get through the door the room repeats and I can't leave. I'm having a mental breakdown. "Let me out, please! Someone, please help. I'm scared. Why does there have to be so many rooms? Why so many?"

Liam Crawshaw (13)
Chetwynde School, Barrow-In-Furness

THEY'RE THERE!

They're there. They're always there. Do you ever get the feeling that someone is watching you, watching your every move? They're there. In the corner of your eye, the place you never want to look... and I looked.
It started at night, it always does, as the sun had just been completely covered by the looming clouds. It was just me of course, awful things only happen when you're on your own. Remember that. I was safely in my house, or so I thought but whenever you think you're safe is when you are most vulnerable. I know that now.

Hannah Lauderdale (13)
Chetwynde School, Barrow-In-Furness

THE POSSESSED SCHOOLGIRL

I didn't mean to kill them. I wasn't myself; I remember one minute I was a regular schoolgirl, the next, a complete psychopath trying to kill everyone in my path. It was like I was possessed, controlled by something or someone that was more powerful than I could ever imagine or try to overcome. It was weird because I knew exactly what I was doing, just didn't know how to stop myself from doing it. It was like my 'master' was wanting me to achieve something for them and had to kill everyone in my path to do this.

Chloe Birt-Reed (12)
Chetwynde School, Barrow-In-Furness

CLOSING UP

Click.
"That was one of the worst night shifts of my life."
Click.
"I'm about to lock up then I'll be on my way home."
Click.
"I don't know, I just wish that something would happen for once on one of my shifts."
Click.
"It's so hard to stay awake the whole night, there's only so much coffee I can consume before it's considered dangerous."
Bang!
"What was that. Wait I'll call you back."
Creak!
"This isn't funny. Who's there. Whoever's there I suggest you come out now."
"999 what's your emergency?"
"Hello, please send help there's..."
"Sir... Sir."

Conal MacDonald (15)
The Berwickshire High School, Langtongate

RUBBISH RAT REQUIEM

The round ragged rat rumbled around the garbage, rustling black bags and rummaging around emptied cups and broken glass. The rat ran around the bins as a long looming figure cloaked by the night approached with an object clutched between their hands.

The rat reluctantly rushed beneath a pile of rubbish. Sticking out its crooked face, it glanced back and forth. The figure was not to be seen. *Slam.* A long spiked pole crushed cans cowardly.

There it stood, disgust on its face. The rat ran out. The bat collided with the bottles, shattering everything around the rat. Run rascal.

Jamie Turner
The Berwickshire High School, Langtongate

A HAND

This is the last time I am getting changed in a public bathroom. The depressing cubicle, flickering lights and creaky locks. "Shoot," I whisper as my lipstick clinks against the stone floor, runs out of my bag and under the door. "It's fine I'll get it later." Why am I talking? There's no one here. Something freezing bumps against my foot. My lipstick. I crouch down and peek under the door, nothing. My heart, racing, it's trying to escape out of its skin cage. The slight creak of the door causes my head to jerk up suddenly. A hand.

Abby Rosher
The Berwickshire High School, Langtongate

UNHOLY NUN

The tattered floorboards creaked as I crept towards the tall clock that surveilled the empty passageway. The lonesome tick of the clock that echoed through the church was interrupted by a soft voice, crying for help. From inside the clock? Inch by inch the clock face opened. The numbers written in Roman numerals plummeted to the ground, one by one revealing the words, found you. As I turned around I could feel a distinct burning sensation in my chest. *I have to escape*, I thought, but it was too late, I was already ensnared in the demon nun's hands.

Daniel Adeosun
The Berwickshire High School, Langtongate

IMAGINARY FRIEND

My daughter has an imaginary friend. She talks to him all the time but of course, he's not really there. She tells me that he's real and that he's a bit strange. I play along to keep her happy but I know he's not real.

I hear noises. A man. That's who I see in her room. He is holding a knife, he has a mask over his face. I slowly walk into my daughter's room to see blood trailing under the bed. A hand reaches out from her bed, covered in blood.

"I told you he was real Mummy."

Circe Miller (14)
The Berwickshire High School, Langtongate

YoungWriters®
— Est. 1991 —

YOUNG WRITERS
INFORMATION

We hope you have enjoyed reading this book – and
that you will continue to in the coming years.

If you're a young writer who enjoys reading and creative
writing, or the parent of an enthusiastic poet or story writer,
visit our website **www.youngwriters.co.uk/subscribe** to join
the World of Young Writers and receive news, competitions,
writing challenges, tips, articles and giveaways! There
is lots to keep budding writers motivated to write!

If you would like to order further copies of this book,
or any of our other titles, then please give us a
call or order via your online account.

Young Writers
Remus House
Coltsfoot Drive
Peterborough
PE2 9BF
(01733) 890066
info@youngwriters.co.uk

Join in the conversation!
Tips, news, giveaways and much more!

 YoungWritersUK    YoungWritersCW    youngwriterscw